No hablo Inglés

Andonia Moreno's Sensual Tale Of Language & Love

A Spanish-American
Romance Novel By

MIMI BURBANK

DEDICATION

This book is dedicated to those who have spoken love beyond their native tongue. Please remember to leave a 5-star review if you enjoyed my book!

CONTENTS

ACKNOWLEDGMENTS

I'd like to thank my editor, Erika, for helping me put this book together. I couldn't have done this alone! Thank you Erika!

This book goes out to people with a heart who want to feel love <3

Please enjoy!

1 CHAPTER ONE

Jonas Brandon trudged across the Easthampton Bridge hastily.
Jogging had long been a daily ritual, a means to an end; something to
clear his head when all the fogginess reared up.

He stopped at the other end of the bridge to catch his breath, beads
of sweat cascaded down his face matting his deep brown hair to his
head.

It was something to be grateful for, Jonas thought to himself as he
dislodged the headphone which was directly connected to his
smartphone. He had been listening to the radio -- the disc jockey had
just switched to another song, something that sounded like a cross
between rock & roll and funk.

His breathing, which had been heavy, slowly receded. Running
always brought that on for him. It was almost like some kind of
catalyst, an avenue to forget things which ought to be forgotten, and
Jonas had a lot of things he wanted to forget.

Things which he had simply shut out. However, those things still
haunted him, though, at night -- and even in the office where he
worked as an auditor.

Years had rolled by since his marriage with Melissa had ended. Time was a really funny concept because even though the years piled up like empty disposed cans, the memories still lingered. Clutching at his very sanity were the bitter pangs of regret and pain which only made such memories worse.

He had met Melissa when he had only just graduated from Greenville Institute of Business Management, which was situated in the heart of Fairfield, North Carolina. Of course, Jonas had never considered himself to be very good-looking or dashy.

He tried as much as possible to maintain his weight, which always seemed to creep up on him. He was quite tall but not exactly the muscular hunk you'd see tossing up a martini in a bar on a Saturday evening. But, personally, there was something about his eyes which always seemed to attract the ladies. His eyes were deep blue, as clear as calm sea water, which seemed to melt any girl on her feet. It had sure gotten Melissa.

She was still a sophomore, having gained admission to study Business and Financial Management while Jonas was already in his third year. He had been headed to the gym, which was just on the west side of Greenville, when they had met.

"I think I've seen you around. You're that guy who managed to balance the ledgers for Stroudsburg and Co. back at Professor Sydney's class," Melissa said, regarding him with delight.

Jonas had been taken aback -- just a little bit. "Oh, well," he proceeded cheerfully, "I sure do have my way with numbers."

"I wish I had that knack. But I guess I'm not a natural," Melissa replied smiling.

It was that smile that set him off. That smile was brighter than a thousand suns fused together. It had ignited a passion in him like no other.

"Well, you don't have to be a natural. I could show you a few tricks if you have the time, perhaps over a cup of coffee," Jonas affirmed, smiling back.

"That's a first," Melissa blurted out, quite exasperated.

"How do you mean?" Jonas asked, rather confused. "Is that a NO on my offer?"

Melissa shook her head vigorously; her hair, which was done up in a ponytail, waved back and forth. "I meant, you're the first guy asking me out on a date, which was totally unexpected."

"Oh, why's that?" Jonas asked with genuine interest.

"Nothing, exactly," she said. "I'll see you around." And with that, she was soon hurrying away, and Jonas just watched her go.

"Hey!" he called after her. "You haven't told me your name!" But his voice was only lost in the evening breeze as she disappeared into the confines of the dormitory.

That had been his first encounter with Melissa Whiteshell. And it had left him absolutely astounded.

He had spent the night thinking about her -- hoping that, somehow, he could get to see her again. And as it turned out, he had gotten to see her about three weeks later at the gym.

The gym, which was located in downtown Claremont, was probably the biggest in Fairfield. It was host to so many people, especially students from Greenville who strutted in and out to work out. Jonas had always been a regular at the gym, mostly because he was trying to burn off some calories that had amassed as a result of his junk diet.

Then he caught sight of her again. This time, the urge had grown stronger -- perhaps, even more intense. She was clad in yoga pants over a tight singlet, which seemed to hug her upper frame tightly, and her hair was held back with a band, which showed off her straight neck.

She was doing sit-ups, completely oblivious of his presence. Jonas had just stood there enraptured, captivated and enveloped in wonder as he watched her. For a few seconds, he was even aware that he wasn't breathing until her eyes finally connected with his and she had flashed him that warm smile again.

His chest tightened and air whooshed out of him quickly. She was standing up and headed towards him, using a napkin to wipe the perspiration that had formed on her forehead.

"Hello, never thought I'd see you here," she said.

"I guess fate has a way of bringing us together. That's kind of reflective, don't you think?" Jonas replied.

She guffawed loudly at that. "I'm really sorry about the other day; I guess I owe you some kind of apology. I was being very honest, though; you were the first guy to ask me out."

"It's okay. I don't really mind, I was just getting a little bit too curious about you. And I guess I must satisfy that curiosity now," Jonas stated grinning.

"I thought you were here to work out?" she furthered. "Hope I'm not a distraction."

"Not at all... What's your name?" Jonas asked and added, "You never really gave me a chance to get to know you before you simply bolted away."

She giggled again. "I'm Melissa, Melissa Whiteshell, or if you're trying to get in my bad books, you can call me Mel for short."

"Your bad books...? You hate having your name abbreviated?"

"Certainly, it really sucks."

"I guess I'd have to remember that. I'm Jonas Brandon," Jonas declared, extending his right hand towards her. She shook it briefly and smiled again.

"So, are you still gonna stall on my offer? Or are you gonna accept it?" Jonas asked.

And that had been it. Their love story had known no bounds; it was almost like a dream out of some fairytale.

By the time he had finally graduated from Greenville with upper honors, Melissa was in her penultimate year. And on the night of her graduation, Jonas had knelt down in a restaurant, which was close to the school, amidst lighted candles, a floor scattered with roses, bottles of expensive wine and proposed to her. The ring was unique. It had actually belonged to his grandmother; it had a gold band with a real diamond stone.

Melissa had simply cried and knelt with him; the restaurant was agog with the applause of everyone who had watched the spectacular proposal that Jonas had pulled off. It had been one of the most glorious moments of his life.

But all that was in the past now, forgotten like chaff scattered in the wind. He and Melissa had gotten married. It had been one of those perfect marriages, and it had lasted for about three years until things started going downhill.

First, it had started with his drinking habit. Even though he had always considered himself to be a social drinker, Jonas knew that there was something in him that would eventually snap and give in one day -- something which he had gotten from his father.

Alistair Brandon, who majorly worked as an orderly back in the 1970s, was a heavy drinker. Well, in a way, you couldn't exactly blame the old man. He was a widower with three boys to cater for, and Jonas had been the youngest. There were times when he had seen his father hobble up the front porch with a bottle of Scotch still in his grip, swaying this way and that before finally collapsing on the floor.

His older brothers, Mason and Kye, would then help in carrying his father back into the house. It was always a trying time, because sometimes their father didn't stay asleep.

During such nights of drunken wonder, he would sometimes lash out at his sons, get a little violent at Mason or Kye and hurl things at them, while Jonas himself cringed back behind his brothers in fear. With his tantrums done, he would collapse on the floor spurting out loads of vomit.

His brothers never complained. They would carry Father back to bed, change his clothes and clean up the vomit which was spattered on the linoleum floor.

Those years had made Jonas scared; he never wanted to end up like his father, and he had solemnly promised himself that. But things were always bound to change one way or the other. And that change had occurred when he met Rick.

Rick Shaw had turned out to be one of his most trusted friends. For Jonas, having friends was just another overrated concept. But that notion had changed when he met Rick, who turned out to be an associate with Price and Bobson, which happened to be the financial firm that Jonas was working in at the time. If there was anything that Rick had, it was money, lots of it. Money that could buy anything. Rick had loads of it.

They had met during one of the many meetings which the firm had arranged. Rick was hiring the firm to help in auditing his company's accounts, and they had put Jonas on the job. It had turned out to be rather successful, and Jonas uncovered huge amounts of money which were being siphoned during shady business deals. Rick had been more than impressed.

"What do you say, mate?" Rick had started. "Let me buy you a drink sometime."

"Thanks a lot, Mr. Shaw, but I'll take a rain check, perhaps another time," Jonas had replied calmly.

"A rain check…? Now, that's new. A man who doesn't drink," Rick chuckled. "Anyway, I'd really like you to stop by sometime. If you think you can handle a glass of martini or two, meet me at the Red Bull," Rick added, winking at him.

Jonas had had no intention whatsoever to honor that invitation, but somehow, after work, had found himself amidst lots of people and loud metal music.

The Red Bull was actually the club to be. Strippers danced, rolling around shiny poles; whiffs of smoke and crack clouded the air, and Jonas could make out Rick in the VIP section of the club surrounded by girls and two bodyguards.

"Hey, Jonas, how are you doing, my friend?" Rick's voice was jovial as Jonas made his way, ushered in by two bodyguards, towards him.

"Fine, well, I can't spend too much time here. My wife is kind of used to me getting home early," Jonas had said.

"Wife…? You're married, bro? Oh, that's a shame. But good for you. Anyway, not to worry, I don't intend to keep you all night," Rick replied, puffing on a lighted cigar; a lady in a black lingerie was caressing his beard slowly.

"Thanks, so why did you insist I have a drink with you?" Jonas asked.

"C'mon, Jonas, don't be so up-tight. Have a drink. Busboy!" Rick shouted at the top of his voice. A scrawny looking man with a Red Sox baseball cap hurried towards their table. Jonas settled for a glass of martini. Well, he had figured that having just one glass wasn't going to really hurt, anyway. So long he didn't have to turn up drunk.

"I really like you, Jonas; I hope we can be real close buddies. You're smart and I could use a smart friend; all I have around me are blockheads," Rick grunted, almost choking on his tequila, which he took with one quick swig.

"Thanks, Rick. But I really have to get going. It's getting quite late," Jonas had blurted out hastily, but Rick was not going to have that.

In the end, they had ended up rather drunk, with Jonas having a go at three strippers. Ever since he had gotten married to Melissa, his life had been cut short from fun. It was not that he wasn't enjoying the marriage, but everything seemed to be mechanical. He went to work, ate his lunch, got back home and ate dinner. And if he was lucky enough, he and Mel would have sex if she wasn't tired or fagged out from her work at the bank.

His life had turned out to be cyclical, but Rick freed him, and that was when things went bad.

She nagged him constantly each day he came back from office a little tipsy. He had endured it at first, but as time went on, it started to piss him off.

"Why do you keep doing this, Jonas?" Melissa would ask silently. "You never used to drink; I guess this Rick guy must be a bad influence."

"Nope… Rick's a great guy. If you can't see that, I guess it's because you just don't want to," Jonas always replied.

"All I'm saying is, just take it easy. I know we have been kind of saddled down with work lately, but still -- I just wish you could stop this bad habit. It's not healthy," Melissa said.

"Perhaps that would have been easier if we could come around to having children," Jonas muttered. They had been trying for the past few months to no avail, and it had only gotten worse.

Jonas didn't know. But he had that queasy feeling that part of it was what was actually contributing to his very recent behavior. Although, this was something he didn't mention to Mel.

"Are you blaming me?" she asked. Jonas could hear the hurt in her voice; it was almost like eating a bunch of stones. It gritted against his being.

"No. I'm not blaming you," his voice was almost a whisper. "All I'm saying is, I'm trying to deal with this in my own way."

"You'll never achieve that by drinking yourself to stupor every other night, Jonas, and you know it," she replied, turning to leave him standing in the living room of their ramshackle bungalow on Pine's Avenue.

He knew he had hurt her, but was he really to blame? He was rather tired, tired of the boredom. And even though Jonas knew that Rick was honestly a bad influence on him, that didn't deter him from drinking with the guy anyway, at least he never even had to pay for the drinks.

Things eventually came to a head when something really bad happened -- something which made Melissa hate him.

He had been to the Red Bull with Rick, as usual, and after their drinking spree, which had gone on for almost six hours, he and Rick had hopped into his newly acquired Rolls-Royce and headed for Wickham Pass, which directly intersected Pine's Avenue.

The ride back home had been surprisingly smooth and devoid of anything untoward. He and Rick had been singing to Billy Farrell's

Sing for Me Stranger album when Rick had lost total control of the car and crashed the mailbox directly in front of Jonas' house.

They had both alighted from the car and hollered loudly, seeing the wreck that they had wrought. And that was when Melissa, who had been awake all night waiting for him, opened the door and stepped outside.

She had been waiting patiently for him to get back so she could break the news to him. Minutes had turned into hours, and yet, Jonas hadn't showed up. What they had been hoping for had finally happened. She was pregnant, and she had wanted it to be a surprise for him.

Seeing her, Jonas and Rick only guffawed even more loudly. "Hey, babe, what are you still doing up? Lost your way in the house? Or perhaps you're sleepwalking again."

"You're drunk, again." Her voice felt like cold steel which plunged through his skin; he could hear the disappointment therein, and it was pissing him off.

"Meet my friend Rick. Rick, here's my beautiful wife, Melissa," Jonas said, dragging Rick along with him.

"Happy to make your acquaintance, Mrs. Brandon. Jonas has told me--" Rick started but Melissa's hand went up cutting him short.

"Save it, Rick, I've heard all about you, and I want you to stay away from my husband. You're making him do things he wouldn't do. Please, can you leave now?" Melissa was angry; there was absolutely no doubt about it.

"C'mon, Mel, don't be such a bitch," Jonas urged and tried to touch her, and that earned him a sound slap across the face.

Jonas put his hand slowly to his face and stared at his wife in blind rage, and that was when everything went blank.

The last thing he could remember was Rick trying to get him off her; there was blood everywhere. Blood which seemed like a little red pond.

The ambulance had come, and somehow, they had managed to sell the story that Melissa had had some kind of freak accident while she and Jonas were having an argument.

She was unconscious for days, and Jonas had wept like a baby when the doctor had informed him that she had actually been pregnant.

After she had gotten out of the coma, she had been hysterical, stating that she didn't want to see him. He was suddenly a hideous monster to her.

"Jonas, buddy, we're never drinking again," Rick said seriously as they both sat outside his front porch. Somehow, he couldn't bring himself to be angry at Rick. After all, it was he who had beaten his own wife to a pulp. Not Rick.

"I guess so, but what I don't really get is why she won't see me?" Jonas muttered sadly, tears streaked down his face.

"She's still in shock. I guess she'll never recover from it," Rick replied, looking away.

"But, why did I do that to her? Why? I don't even remember how I snapped out. And our baby..." His shoulders shook with grief, and he wailed loudly.

Rick had managed to put him to bed, and for days things just seemed strange and surreal. And no matter how much he tried -- the guilt was there.

Melissa was discharged after three weeks, but she didn't come back home to him; she went to her mother's in Chicago. And not for one day did she speak to him again. The divorce papers arrived via mail, and Jonas had stared at it hazily.

It all seemed like some kind of dream, something out of a movie or a book which had a tragic ending. With shaky hands, he had held the divorce papers and scanned it thoroughly.

The papers had glided down to the floor from his wanton grip and he had slumped to the ground.

Days passed and he finally resigned from Price and Bobson. Rick urged him not to leave the job, but Jonas' mind was made up. He sold the apartment and finally signed the divorce papers.

He was going to start over again and forget everything he had done wrong. It wouldn't be easy, but he was going to at least try.

Rick offered him a part-time job as an accountant, which he had taken up, and he had simply allowed himself to float through life.

Jonas straightened up; he was looking out at the calm river, which shimmered in the morning sun, with his hands gripping at the rails of the bridge.

Those were the things he had tried to forget. Things that made him lose sleep at night, things that had made him broken. He had not heard from Melissa in years since the divorce, and he didn't blame her. She had been more than anything he could hope for.

Perhaps, he would have another chance, but Jonas knew that it would certainly not be with her anymore.

The sound of heavy shuffling footfalls jolted him out of his silent reverie. A figure was jogging towards his direction, and even though the rays of the rising sun, which was just overhead, seemed to obscure the face, Jonas knew it was a woman.

As the figure drew closer, he could make out distinctive features; she was not quite tall, her legs seemed as strong as an oak tree and her hair, which was deep black and curly, fell in graceful tresses behind her back. Her hair bobbed up and down, and Jonas could see that her breathing made her firm breasts heave up.

Her eyes caught him staring as she drew closer across the bridge, and Jonas averted his gaze quickly, but she smiled at him. From his own deduction, she was certainly not American or at least she didn't look it. But that was none of his business, he reasoned.

Jonas watched her go; there was something about her that reminded him of Melissa, something which seemed too hard to explain in words. Her silhouette soon disappeared at the end of the bridge which led directly to the park.

He sighed heavily, reconnected his headphones and turned on the smartphone. There was a text from Rick, who had been true to his word as regards their early drinking habits:

Hiya Jonnyboy, I was thinking, wanna hit the lake with me this weekend? I'm going fishing and I sure could use some companionship! C'mon, don't tell me no. Life's gotta move on, let's enjoy ourselves! If you agree to come, we'll take the yacht (I know you're still nursing a strong desire to ride it!)

P.S: I might be also inviting some friends over.

Jonas glanced at the text and smiled. Rick had always been one for surprises. Even though he'd never admit it, Jonas knew that Rick was still feeling as guilty as he felt about the incident of that night, but there was nothing either of them could do to change the past.

Music blared into his ears, a song by Judas Priest that Jonas wasn't quite familiar with:

Take off and fly

Gotta turn this party round,

So many roads ahead to ply,

13

Gotta turn this party around.

He resumed jogging, somehow; the face of the lady he had seen just across the bridge slipped into his mind. Her eyes were like beautiful pearls which seemed to search into the very depths of his soul, and he wondered in spite of himself if he would actually ever see her again. She had not looked like an American anyway, so the possibility of that was actually very slim.

He checked his wristwatch, it was almost 8:45 am, chuckling silently to himself, and he wondered if he could actually head to the office at this time if he was still with Price & Bobson. But that was the many advantages of life, something gets taken away and another gets replaced, a tit for tat.

He was soon in the park and headed towards his new apartment in Claremont. As he bypassed the academic grounds of Greenville, which had once been his school, a feeling of nostalgia descended upon him, but he shrugged it off and tried to concentrate on the people he whizzed past.

Home was just a few blocks away, and yet, the image of the Not-American girl rose up somewhere at the back of his mind. He didn't dismiss this particular picture. Life was, after all, about second chances, and Jonas knew he had to forgive himself and have that second chance.

But what he didn't envisage was how quick he got that chance, which set things in motion in the days to come.

2 CHAPTER TWO

"C'mon pull it in!" Rick screamed excitedly. "Don't tell me you're scared of a trout," he added.

Jonas only shook his head; it was indeed turning out to be a great weekend. Accepting Rick's offer had been a rather wise choice. They were presently on Rick's yacht, which he called "The Anchor." It was a fairly large luxury boat; there were about five mini-like cabins, a bar, and even a small basketball court. Jonas had agreed to navigate the boat, which was now presently on the Lake Fargo, and headed back to shore.

"Damn, she's a beauty," Rick said suddenly. "Just look at her, all shiny and looking like some glorified mermaid from an Aesop fable."

"Well, I gotta hand it to you, Rick, she's sure fine," Jonas replied, still twirling around the line of his fishing rod. He had failed to bring in another trout, and that had been the whole point of the expedition.

"Ain't talking about the boat, stupid. Look at the shore," Rick said pointing.

Jonas dropped his fishing rod slowly and started up; the yacht, which had been set to auto-navigation, cruised on the lake. Just ahead, Jonas could make out dozens of people on the shore, but following Rick's finger, he could see that he was pointing at a woman. And there was something about her poise that seemed so familiar to Jonas.

"Fine, ain't she?" Rick's voice cut through his thoughts. "Perhaps we should consider giving her a ride."

"I don't know about that. But I think I know her," Jonas muttered under his breath.

"What did you say?" Rick asked.

"I think I might know her, but I just can't really remember where, at the moment," Jonas repeated. The woman at the shore side was not too tall, and her curly black hair was being flared up by the rushing wind. She was clad in a bikini, which was hidden by a wrap-around sarong scarf tied and double knotted at the hip.

"C'mon, Jonas, don't fuck with me, man. How would you know her? Most of the folks out here are Mexicans; they often come out here for their weekend lake parties," Rick noted.

"Well, I could be wrong, but I don't think my memory has ever disappointed. I could also be right, though. She sure looks like someone I know," Jonas asserted.

"Alright, perhaps we should just hit the other side and see if you can get a clearer view," Rick suggested, and Jonas only nodded his head slowly. He went over to the navigator's cabin and directed the boat towards the port.

After the yacht was safely in place, both men alighted. Jonas was still staring at the Mexican lady, but she hadn't quite noticed him yet.

The other side of the lake was crowded with people, there were kids playing with shells and stones, while some others were busy hunting for crabs. Music boomed from a loud speaker, which seemed rather broken; the sound was totally distorted.

"Okay, here's your chance, buddy. Good luck. I'll see if I can grab a canned beer or something," Rick whispered into his ear and Jonas shook his head.

"I thought we were done drinking?" he asked sarcastically.

"Oh, well, I guess I could use a beer right now," Rick grunted and walked off towards a small bar at the entrance to the lake.

Jonas stood for a while from a distance, watching her. The urge to approach her was strong, but he dismissed this quickly.

She had to be the one he had seen on the Easthampton Bridge. There was no mistake. The hair and the poise were exactly as it had been, and here she was, watching the sunset go down.

While he still contemplated going to meet her, she turned around, caught him looking and started towards him.

He had seen her coming and had been quick to avert his gaze away, not wanting to see her move towards him. Perchance, she was headed back to her tent or whatever it was she was going back to, but certainly not to him.

"Hola…?" she said. Her voice quite pure and tranquil, almost like warm milk on a freezing night.

"Uhmm… Hi," Jonas heard himself say. She was standing right in front of him, looking so graceful.

"I see you at bridge, que onda?" she furthered.

"Yeah, I guess so, I saw you sometime back on the Easthampton Bridge, and you were jogging. I was just wondering if you were the one," Jonas said.

She nodded her head briskly, and suddenly fell silent still looking at him, so he said: "I'm Jonas Brandon, so what's your name?"

No reply came forth, she only moped at him. And suddenly, he realized that, perhaps, she didn't understand what he had meant. She just stood looking at him, perhaps still expecting him to introduce himself further.

"I meant, I'm Jonas Brandon," he gesticulated, placing both hands on his chest before pointing at her, "WHAT IS YOUR NAME?"

"Oh, yo soy Andonia Moreno," she replied smiling.

"What's that?" Jonas asked, rather confused.

She pointed to herself and gesticulated, imitating what he had done initially when he was introducing himself.

"Your name is Andonia Moreno?" he asked, suddenly catching on what she had meant.

She nodded her head vigorously in agreement and said, "No hablo Inglés."

Jonas only looked on at her in confusion, to be honest; he had never ever deemed it fit to actually know how to speak the Mexican language. It didn't matter that most of his buddies back in college had actually been Mexicans. It hadn't really mattered then. After all, they were equally as educated as he was and saw no need for the language.

"I mean, don't know English," Andonia furthered, seeing the confusion scribbled on Jonas' face.

"Oh, I thought as much. So, do you jog often?" he asked, indicating what he meant by running in one spot.

She nodded her head sharply and smiled, which almost melted Jonas' heart. Her teeth were white and quite perfect; well set and ivory like. "Si."

"I guess that means a Yes. Do you think we could go jogging

sometime? I've been looking for a partner, and I'm really starting to get all old and stuck up," he added.

"Si, I love to," Andonia replied, which was much to the relief of Jonas because he was starting to honestly wonder if he had simply rambled on.

"That's gonna be gre--" a large hand landed on his back, and he whirled around to see Rick standing with a can of beer in his hand, grinning wildly.

"What do we have here?" Rick declared laughingly. "Who's this lovely damsel?"

"C'mon, Rick, be nice. This is Andonia, I told you I kinda knew her. Remember that day I told you I was jogging on the Easthampton Bridge? Well, she's the one who jogged past me."

Andonia smiled and extended her hand towards Rick. "Buenas noches, nice to meet you."

"Nice to meet you too. She's sure fine, Jonas. Have fun, just got a call from Larry," Rick said, hastily patting Jonas on the back. "See you back at the house." And with that, Rick trudged along hastily.

"That was my friend," Jonas affirmed, pointing at Rick.

Andonia nodded her head, indicating that she understood. Even though she couldn't quite comprehend some of the more complex English words, she still found it easy to absorb the simpler ones.

Jonas plunged his hand to his jeans pocket and took out his smartphone, "Can I have your cell phone number?" he asked slowly. "So I can call you at my convenient time."

"Oh, cell phone?" she asked bemused. And just when Jonas was thinking she probably didn't comprehend what he was trying to tell her, she hurried off towards one of the erected tents and came back with a cell phone.

Surprisingly, she took his phone and punched in her number quickly before handing it back to him. "You call me?"

"Sure," Jonas beamed with a smile. "I sure will, Andonia. It's been nice talking to you. I guess I have to go now."

"Hasta luego, Jonas," she whispered softly as Jonas took her hands into his own. A kind of electric feeling -- something that he hadn't felt in a long time since his divorce with Melissa -- passed through him.

"I guess that means goodbye," he replied. "I sure do hope you'll remember me when I call," he added mildly.

She only nodded her head, smiled at him again and walked off back to the tent. Jonas watched her go, a sudden urge to rush and grab her almost numbed his senses, but he stood his ground anyway with the breeze ruffling his disheveled hair. After he was sure she was completely gone, he turned around and left the lakeside.

* * *

"So, how did it go with your new Mexican girlfriend?" Rick teased. "She's hot. I'll give her that." They were presently back at Rick's condo in Claremont, which was directly overlooking Pine's Avenue.

"Come off it, Rick, I hardly know her. Besides, I noticed she had great difficulty in speaking English," Jonas noted thoughtfully.

"That's the case with most inbred Spanish Mexicans, man. They can hardly communicate in any other language except their own," Rick said, opening a can of Diet Coke.

"So, most of them can't speak English? That's kind of crazy, Mexico is hardly far off from America," Jonas protested.

"You'll understand what I mean as time goes on, bro. Only time will tell, but sex doesn't really need any sort of complex communication, just show her the dick," Rick chuckled loudly at that.

"Point to your head and say Mark Twain's initials, buddy, that's right. What a dumb thing to say," Jonas grunted. "I'm actually looking for something more from her, not just petty sex."

"Are you for real?" Rick asked, suddenly serious. "Like for real, REAL?"

"Of course. I got her phone number too, I guess that counts for something. I just, honestly, hope she'll remember me," Jonas said reflectively. That was his only fear. He had seen the way she was lost when he tried to introduce himself in the afternoon. It had taken her some effort, which he had been very patient to observe.

"But I thought you just wanted to get down with her. Besides, she's really good, but how would you communicate with her?" An expression of astonishment had scrambled up his features.

"I guess I'll have to just try. I'm very serious. I really like that girl," Jonas said, plopping down on a cushion which was overlooking the fireplace.

Rick nodded in understanding. "I think that's a good thing. I have never seen you serious about women since Mel, and it kind of gets me down," a hint of sadness had encroached his voice.

"Hey, no need going down memory lane. I absolutely understand what you mean," Jonas asserted.

"I know, but there's hardly any day that doesn't pass with me not feeling a bit guilty. If I hadn't taken you to the bar that day--" Rick continued, but Jonas cut him short.

"That's enough, Rick, none of what happened was your fault. I have long stopped blaming people, and I have taken responsibility for my actions."

"Go for her, Jonas. Perhaps she'll lead you back to the light."

"Of course, I don't know why I feel so excited just thinking about her, but I sure won't pass up the chance. Thanks, Rick."

"You're welcome, man. Wanna play a game of chess?"

After their brief chess game had ended, with Rick winning at least three games in a row, they retired to bed.

Jonas had agreed on Rick's request to spend the night over instead of having to ride home.

Before sleep eluded him, all he could think of was that beautiful smile, that deep black hair which smelt like a combination of roses and lilies lumped up together. It was the best feeling that he had had in a very long time. Before he slipped away into oblivion, he made a mental note to contact her as soon as soon as possible.

* * *

Work at the office had proceeded in a timely fashion. Most of the paperwork, which he had been rooting to do the week before but never really came around to doing, were all done quickly.

A new lease of energy had descended upon him and he wondered where that energy had emanated from. Previously, he had lost almost all interest in his career as an accountant and auditor. But today, today was quite different.

"You seem rather different today," Susan Fell observed. She had been his secretary for almost two years, since Jonas had taken up the position in Rick's firm. "I don't mean to intrude, but it's glaring all over you."

Jonas gawped at her in shock. "That's really not true. I'm just in a very good mood is all." His hands flipped through the papers quickly in a methodical manner.

"Well, what I see is more than just being in a good mood. I'm your personal secretary, Mr. Jonas. I have watched and studied you for almost two years now, and I know something really great has happened," Susan furthered; there was a mischievous grin on her face.

"Honestly, I have no idea what you're talking about. Please, kindly forward the financial statement and balance sheet for the Rodgers account. We have to have that work cleared out before noon," Jonas instructed, quickly changing the subject.

"Alright, sir," Susan affirmed before heading out of the office.

Women were quite telepathic. He had to hand them that. Damn, even Susan had noticed the obvious change in his demeanor. Jonas wondered if this was as a result of him thinking about Andonia, who he still hadn't called for about three days.

It wasn't like he didn't want to call her, but he had been deliberately stalling on it. Yet, the feeling had grown only stronger by day; he needed to talk to her one way or the other.

He glanced at his smartphone and picked it up slowly. Then he clicked on the contact list and Andonia's name popped up. He tapped on the call button and suddenly disconnected it again.

The only feeling that he had was that, if she eventually did answer her phone, she would not remember him or she'd find it difficult to understand if he asked her out to dinner.

He picked up the smartphone again, quite undecided, and redialed the number. It rang for some time, which was clearly indicated by the dial tone which beeped over and over, before finally going to her voicemail, which Jonas didn't bother to hear. He had ended the call.

3 CHAPTER THREE

She had waited patiently for his call. Being patient was one of the traits that Andonia possessed; her mother had often told her she had gotten the virtue from her *abuela*. Of course, she had known that he would come; it had been like being able to see into the future.

The connection she had felt ever since she had first seen him on the Easthampton Bridge had been immediate and intense. So intense that she had spent the night thinking about him, and yet, she knew he was American. And she knew how her pappy loathed Americans.

"Americans, pinche perros!" her father would always exclaim when he talked about how the Americans brutalized them during the years just before the Civil Rights Act bill was passed. "They fucking crazy! And heartless!"

But Jonas hadn't looked heartless; he had seemed so sweet and maybe even romantic. She could remember as he had taken so much time and effort to ensure that he could tell her his name, and also get to know hers. It was something that she hadn't forgotten as she replayed that scenario over and over in her mind.

His deep blue eyes had melted her soul and seared through like burning fire into the very depths of her spirit. And when he had offered to jog with her, she had felt a kind of warm feeling -- and this had never happened with even her first love, Diego.

She hoped silently that he would call. There was also the urge to call him first, but she didn't want to be misunderstood. Even though she knew that deep down Jonas was good, she also knew he was still a man. And men would seize on whatever opportunity to bluster their ego.

So, she had waited patiently, looking at her cell phone after every hour to ensure that she had not missed his call, but no call came through.

"Andonia…?" The voice of her mother startled her out of her thoughts. All of a sudden, she realized that she was still in the kitchen back in the restaurant, which was owned by her uncle.

The smell of roasted turkey wafted into her nostrils, and she soon realized why her mother had been calling her, "Un momento por favor, los siento!" she shouted back.

"Andale…! Andonia, customers waiting!" her mother replied back, which made her quite jittery. Her mother was one for having things done in a quick fashion, especially now that they worked for her uncle, Antonio.

She took out the roasted turkey from the oven and proceeded to slice it hastily. After she was done garnishing it up, she passed it quickly to her another chef, who dressed it and went to serve the order. She glanced at her cell phone, which was still on the kitchen table, for one last time and headed towards the freezer for another turkey. That was when her phone vibrated and showed an incoming call from: JONAS.

* * *

There was every possibility that she had seen that call and ignored it.

It was not impossible. After all, there was bound to be some kind of insecurity if they couldn't exactly communicate well with each other. But he didn't want to hold onto that notion. She hadn't seemed to be that type of person; although, this was something he wasn't entirely sure of.

Glancing down at his phone again, Jonas decided to call just one more time -- he had to be double sure.

He redialed again.

And this time, it was quite different. Her voice, which had nearly almost melted his heart like a piece of steel put through burning fire, was cheerful and bright.

"Hallo? Buenas noches."

"How are you doing, Andonia? This is Jonas. I called about some minutes ago," Jonas replied hastily. Suddenly, his voice was rather shaky, and somewhat laced with fear.

"Sale si," she muttered. "I working at time."

"I don't really get what you mean," Jonas chipped in, quite confused. What he could deduce from what she had said was just 'working' and 'time.'

"Working," she simply repeated again.

"Oh, you were working?" Jonas asked.

"Si. Work at restaurante."

Jonas tried to absorb and comprehend that before replying to her, "You work in a restaurant?"

"Si. With Madre," she replied.

"I think I have heard that word a few times before, that's 'mother,' right?" Jonas furthered.

He heard her chuckle a little, before affirming that he was indeed right. So, he had found out that she was working in a restaurant with her mother, at least from what he could deduce so far.

"Well, I just wanted to ask if you'd like to have dinner with me sometime. I don't know if it's too early or too late, but I just felt I should as--" Jonas rambled on. There was the fear of the fact that she could actually refuse, and also the fear that she would not quite understand what he meant by dinner.

"Si," was her simple reply. And he didn't have to understand Mexican for him to really know that she had agreed to have dinner with him.

"Wow. That was really quick, didn't have to convince you so much," he said.

She giggled lightly. "Dinner…? I know dinner," she added reflectively.

"Great. So what time are you free? Perhaps, around 8:00pm tomorrow night should do, at the Grand Royale in Claremont. I'll pick you up," Jonas said. "You reside at Hovels March just across the lake, right?" he added swiftly.

"Si, Hovels March," she responded.

"Okay, I guess we have a date then," his voice sounded jocund. It had to be, this was the opportunity.

"De acuerdo, gracias, Jonas. Adios," she blurted out hastily and cut the call.

Jonas gawped at his phone for a few minutes to be sure that the call had actually ended. Of course, it had. At the end of their conversation, he had sensed an urgency which had not been there before. She had not been in a haste initially, perhaps something came up, Jonas reasoned, smiling. But the most important thing was that she had agreed to his offer for dinner.

With a sudden burst of energy, Jonas stood up and swaggered towards the door of the office. Definitely, he had to inform Rick.

* * *

Mother's voice had disrupted her flow of thoughts, dislodged her from the little magical moment that she had been having with Jonas and brought her back to reality.

She had not noticed her mother's presence due to the fact that her back had been turned all the while as she chatted on the phone.

Her mother's voice had cut through her thoughts like a knife through shea butter.

"Andonia…?"

She whirled around sharply to find her mother standing at the other end of the kitchen counter, which was directly almost past the refrigerator.

"Madre..." her voice was almost a whisper. She knew her mother had probably heard most of her conversation with Jonas, and her parents really loathed Americans. "Que es la que hay…?"

"Andonia, Pilas! Americans es muy fresa. Bad for you," her mother chided in a bitter and cold tone.

"Madre, Jonas is good," Andonia said quietly, "Not like Diego."

But her mother only hissed and left her standing in the kitchen with her phone still held tightly in her grip.

It was not totally unexpected. Her parents loathed Americans, like every other core Mexican. There was the general belief that

Americans were totally stuck up, haughty and proud. This was the major reason why they did business in the areas of the town which were majorly occupied by Mexicans.

That was the general notion. But Andonia knew better. Well, it was not that she hadn't received her own fair share of insults hurled at her every single time that they had an American customer, which was often rare, but she believed that this man wasn't like that.

And she honestly hoped to God that she was right. There was the fact that he couldn't speak Mexican Spanish, and there was also the fact that he wasn't going to be able to conform easily to certain norms that she had been taught throughout her childhood. She shrugged and headed towards the oven to take out the next order of macaroni and cheese. At least there was an upside to it; she would soon be having dinner with him.

4 CHAPTER FOUR

It wasn't exactly a long ride home. It had always been a long drive home, but that wasn't the case for Jonas tonight. He smiled to himself as he sped past Easthampton Bridge, the North Shore Park and headed downtown towards Claremont. It was almost mid-November; humidity levels were quite high, and it was looking like it would snow in less than a month. Whiffs of cold air rushed in and out of his lungs as his right hand turned the steering wheel of his Toyama 67 model.

He bypassed rows of shops, which had already started setting up Christmas lights; a gas station, which was just ahead down in North Shore Park, had a neon light shaped with a no-smoking sign blinking on and off. He brought the car to a halt just as the traffic light overhead down Claremont flickered and changed from green to red.

In a way, the night ride was not long because he was excited. He had never felt such an excitement before, not since Melissa. He chided himself. Why were the feelings that he had for a lady who he barely knew so strong? After all, he had met so many women after his divorce with Melissa. Some of them who knew he was hurting had tried to provide him with comfort, which he had turned down. It wasn't that he couldn't use it then, but he was overwhelmed with grief, grief that had threatened to rip his very heart out of his chest.

He sighed heavily. But Andonia made him excited, she made him forget, and that was quite important. He needed to forget those grim times which would sometimes rear up at the back of his mind like the legendary Hydra, so many heads bobbing up and down, heads that needed to be cut off.

The dinner would be quite perfect, for starters. He would get to know her, perhaps even learn how to speak Mexican Spanish. There were so many things he needed to know, and he hoped he would find out soon enough.

Overhead, the traffic light switched from red to green, and Jonas slammed his feet down on the accelerator. The car lurched forward and took the turning on the left. Activities in the city had long reduced and the evening breeze brought in chills which foreshadowed the oncoming festive season.

* * *

Diego had been her first love and she hated herself now for loving him. He had been everything she had ever wanted in a man. Tall, handsome, with long hair that was soft like the mane of a pony, hands large and rigid like sturdy oak trees; hands that had gotten tough from dragging and carrying bags and bags of coffee, deep grey eyes and a heavily built body.

But he had been lacking in only one thing; something that Andonia craved and hoped in every man: Care and affection. Diego Contaro had none of those things.

"Chinga tu madre…!" he had retorted at her the last time they had met. "Fuck you and fuck your pappy, Andonia."

She had only looked on at him quite unresponsive. When Diego started cussing, it was best that he be left alone. The issue had started when he wanted to sleep with her. This had not been an issue for the years that they had dated, but Diego always placed his own needs before hers.

She had been ill for days with the flu. It had gotten so bad that she had been admitted in the hospital and given several intravenous drips. When she had almost recovered and was due to be discharged from the hospital, she had called Diego.

But even though he knew about her health, he never came. It was typical of Diego, but it really hurt her; and so she had visited him to find out why he didn't come to see her.

"Hey damselo, Que onda?" he said, grinning on seeing her. His body was glistening with sweat that had soaked up his chest, leaving tell-tale splotches on his singlet. There was a huge tattoo on his forearm which looked like the shape of the cross with skulls below.

She had asked him why he didn't visit when she was at the hospital, and he had responded that he had been very busy, which was just a white lie.

"Damselo, te quiero mucho," he whispered under his breath as he moved towards her and used one free hand to cup her breast. She had been wearing a satin blouse over a straight skirt. Looking into his grey eyes, she knew he wanted to have sex with her. It didn't matter to him that she had spent almost seventeen days lying on a hospital bed, nor did it matter to him that she had taken at least five drips on the first day.

All Diego was concerned about the moment he saw her was sex. She slapped his hand off and glared at him angrily.

"Piedra…! Chale…!" she vituperated, making him cringe back in terror. He had made another attempt to kiss her, and then she had slapped him across the face, which was followed by a series of curses and finally -- he hit her on the face.

She had cried for a while, stood up and grabbed her bag before heading for the door. She could still hear him cursing her as she left, but it didn't matter. That was the end of the relationship.

She had totally given up on men. Not that it was something that she had done intentionally, but it had just been instinctive. But on that day on the bridge, something had snapped inside her. Something she couldn't explain.

The Easthampton Bridge had been in sight as she approached it. Jogging had always afforded her some kind of comfort; it allowed her time to think and to gather her thoughts together. And then she had seen him, looking at the calm river just below.

His was the saddest face she had ever seen. She immediately understood that he was lost in deep thought. She hurried across the bridge as the sun came up in full view, and she had seen him. It was strange when she couldn't help smiling at him as he finally turned around to regard her.

His face, which had been sad, had somehow collapsed and was replaced with warmth that she had felt being radiated towards her. And as she went on, she had also hoped to see him again.

And that had come to pass.

Perchance, fate had decided that they were going to eventually talk, and she had seen him again at the lake. It was something that truly baffled her, but it was all in order now. The dinner date would be a perfect way to know him and see if he was the right person for her. She honestly hoped he was.

* * *

He parked his car slowly in the driveway, turned it off and listened to the slow ticking that followed of the engine cooling off. He exhaled deeply and alighted from the car.

The evening breeze sent his shirt flapping like a sailor's sail, and the stars in the dark sky were just starting to show. Even though the light on the front porch was on, the windows of the condo that he shared with Rick were shuttered. Rick was most certainly not at home yet, he thought to himself and stopped short in his tracks.

A shadow was casted on the floor of the porch. Someone whose figure seemed rather familiar, but vague almost at the same time, was seated at the front porch. He blinked his eyes several times to ensure that he wasn't hallucinating and headed towards the figure.

Seated at the foot of the spiral stairs that led up to the condo was Kye. A much older looking Kye. His brother that had once protected him from the drunken tantrums of their father; the one he would hide behind when their father started smashing and throwing stuff around.

Kye stood up and smiled at Jonas as he approached. He was wearing a dog-chain, which had his name engraved on it, and the uniform of the United States Army.

"Kye…? Is this really you?" Jonas asked dreamily.

"Yeah, Jones, in flesh and blood," Kye muttered, still smiling. "How have you been little brother? It's been ages."

No one ever called Jonas "Jones" except Kye Brandon. This was a realization that struck home with so much force that Jonas lunged forward and threw his arms around his brother.

"I can't believe that you are still alive, I just can't believe it," Jonas trumpeted excitedly.

"I did send you postcards. Though, I didn't think I'd survive the Vietnam War, but I actually did and even got promoted. How's your wife? What's her name? Don't tell me. Uhhh… Melissa! You sent me a postcard about the marriage," Kye said.

Jonas' shoulders slumped. "She divorced me, brother, but that's in the past. So much water has passed under this bridge. And I guess the reason why I haven't been getting your postcards was because I sold my house after the divorce and didn't leave my new returning address for the mail company."

"Wow. That's a lot to take in. Now, invite me in. I'm as hungry as fuck," Kye blurted out.

"Sure. C'mon in. It's so nice to see you again. I spoke to Mason about three weeks ago. He's in Philadelphia, making a name for himself with his writing," Jonas said, unlocking the main door.

"I should call him soon too. So, how's work? And life?" Kye asked.

"Fine… Something has been different for days now," Jonas replied as they both stepped into the room.

"Wicked. What a place you have here, bro," Kye complimented, looking around caught up in awe.

"Technically, I don't own this place. I'd have to use all my life savings and insurance to acquire this kind of house, but it belongs to my best friend, Ricky Shaw," Jonas explained.

"Ricky Shaw? That sure rings a bell, though. So, I'm still waiting for the stories, you know I'm a good listener."

"You have always been. But first, we have dinner."

Jonas headed towards the kitchen; there was always a constant supply of groceries, which were quite too much. Rick had an obsession for keeping food and all other basic necessities in excess.

"Just saving for rainy days," he'd say.

"What rainy days? You're a fucking millionaire," Jonas would always reply. He chuckled to himself as he made toast, steak and scrambled eggs.

After the dinner was ready and served. He and Kye ate to their fill and retired back to the fireplace which Jonas started up.

Over bottles of Budweiser, the stories came out in a flurry and Kye listened attentively.

"You know, this kind of reminds me of one of the major reasons why I'm here," Kye started slowly. "Dad's remembrance anniversary is in a few days. I was wondering if we could have a little family reunion and have some pastor say a few words."

Jonas nodded his head in agreement. "Yeah, I guess we could do that."

"I know how you feel about that old man. But trust me, after several years, I started to see things from his perspective. It could have happened to anybody. And from what you just told me about Melissa, it did happen to you too. No one is above mistakes, but the most important thing is taking a few steps back and not repeating them," Kye admonished.

"Yeah, big brother – so, what date do you have in mind for the anniversary?" Jonas asked curiously.

"I was thinking about a few days before Christmas, but whatever, alternate suggestions are still okay. We would still have to call Mason and ask him if it would be convenient for him to fly down," Kye replied.

"Okay. I'd call him tonight," Jonas agreed.

They both fell silent for a while, still sipping their Buds, when Kye asked, "So, this mystery Mexican lady that you just met, how's she like?"

"It's really hard to explain. I'm telling you, you'd probably laugh in my face if I told you," Jonas stated.

"Far from it, I sure won't. I'm just kinda curious, you know? Even as kids, you never really showed any prospect of becoming a hunk in the near future." They both laughed at that.

"Yeah, I was the book guy. But trust me, she totally had me hypnotized. Well, I took to jogging about some months ago, nothing overly draining, but I kept at it to keep in shape and to also take my mind off things. So, I had been jogging just across the bridge when I saw her," Jonas narrated slowly.

"And you talked to her, right?" Kye asked.

"Nope, I just watched her go. I wouldn't have been able to talk to her, though; she was jogging at that time, but she glanced at me and smiled."

"An obvious invitation, which you just blew off," Kye chipped in sarcastically.

"The story hasn't quite ended. So, Rick and I went fishing with this luxury boat he just acquired at the lake, which is opposite Hovels March. And I saw her again. There was something about her as she stood in that open sun looking out at the water; I felt a sudden ecstasy run through me. I navigated the yacht, anchored it and got off. After a few minutes of watching her, she saw me regarding her and headed towards my direction!" Jonas exclaimed excitedly.

"Seriously…? And what did she say?" Kye inquired.

"She affirmed seeing me at the bridge and started speaking Spanish Mexican. Which I, of course, didn't understand."

"She can't speak English?"

"Well, she does try, but she's way used to her mother's tongue. But when she speaks English, it's always in bits," Jonas noted.

"And you don't think that's gonna be a problem, bro?" Kye

furthered.

"I honestly don't know yet. But I really like her. That should count for something, right?"

"Sure. I actually hope it goes well."

"So, I called her recently, and she accepted to have dinner with me tomorrow night. I guess I could, honestly, use that opportunity to know her better," Jonas said.

"Of course, that'd go a long way. Perhaps you could even learn how to speak Mexican from her," Kye grunted.

"You could be right, buddy, and I sure do hope she'll blend in. I wasn't kidding about liking her."

"All and good..." Kye started as the front door swung open and Rick tottered into the room.

"Hey, Rick, meet my brother, Kye," Jonas said, introducing the two men who proceeded to shake hands briefly. The three men soon settled down to more bottles of Buds and watching a basketball game before finally retiring to bed.

5 CHAPTER FIVE

Throughout his day at the office, Jonas' mind was just queasy.
He could hardly have anything meaningful done. All that lingered on
his mind was his meeting with Andonia at exactly 7:45p.m, in time
for dinner, which he hoped would be great.

He considered calling her. But quickly dismissed this thought as
soon as it formed in his head -- he didn't want to appear anxious.
There was not even any sort of assurance that she'd actually be able
to answer his call; she would probably be stuck in the restaurant till
noon, he reasoned thoughtfully.

Since he hadn't been on a date for almost five years, he had taken
his time to get a nice tuxedo in Snips and Cuffs, which was his only
trusted supplier when it came to clothes.

The suit had fit perfectly as he checked himself out in the mirror.
He grinned wildly trying to adjust the bowtie, which he had also
gotten to match with the suit.

Time ticked by slowly, and it was soon almost time for lunch. Most
of the employees took off almost immediately, while Jonas sat back
in the office lost in a reverie, which was actually a daydream of how
his evening would go with Andonia.

"You aren't going to grab a bite, are you?" The voice floated down through his hazy reverie and startled him. He jerked up and glanced to find Susan looking down at him.

"Oh, Suzzy… I'm not particularly hungry, anyway. I just want to actually get back home as soon as possible," Jonas replied, not looking up. He was pretending to shuffle through some papers.

"You're going on a date, aren't you?" Susan smiled.

"Uh...?" Jonas looked on in confusion. How could she have known that? He hadn't even told anyone in the office about his personal life.

"Don't look so flabbergasted. I kinda knew because I saw the three-piece tux holed up in the closet for file storage. It smelt brand new, and I was just wondering why you kept it there, until it fell in place," Susan explained, while Jonas still stared at her wide-eyed. "And note: I wasn't snooping around, I needed to get a file you asked me to treat," she quickly added.

"Okay, you're right. It's just one tiny bitsy date that might not lead to anywhere," he sighed heavily. "But I'm looking forward to it, nevertheless."

"I think it will go just fine, if you push at it," Susan winked at him and headed out of the office towards her cubicle.

Jonas checked his wristwatch; it was nearly 5:45pm. Perhaps, he could grab a bite and head back home to freshen up just in time for the date. According to Rick, going early for the date created a nice impression on the girl, and Jonas needed to make a good point.

* * *

The evening gown was impeccable. It was nothing like she had ever seen. She had seen it after closing from the restaurant -- her mother was still holed up in the other side of the office balancing the accounts for the day. Uncle Antonio didn't joke with his money and always expected a daily turnout, which he had laid quite a lot of emphasis on.

She had been walking home. It had been a long shift, almost about fourteen hours at a stretch for only fifty dollars, which was now well hidden in her purse. Just before the turnpike which led out of Fairfield, and the road which lay out towards Hovels March, she had seen the store.

The sun was travelling fast down the horizon and darkness was beginning to encroach, spreading its tentacles. The store itself, which stood like a loner in an abandoned town, was rather inconspicuous, save for the pink awning which extended out like a protruded belly.

ATILIA'S FASHION HOUSE was inscribed on the awning in green letters and the sign on the door was flipped to OPEN. But what had caught her attention was the evening gown. It was quite simple, and at the same time, very beautiful. The show-glass which housed it glittered like an uncut diamond. And the mannequin, clad in the dress, looked graceful and gorgeous.

She moved closer towards the window and stared at the dress. Yes, this was it, she muttered under her breath. It was a dress quite perfect for a dinner date (not that she had ever been to one).

The dress had long sleeves which extended to the wrists, the hem was flitted, and the color was deep red, almost like crimson.

She exhaled deeply and decided that she was going to have the dress anyway. He would definitely be blown away if he got to see her clad in the dress.

As she made her way into the store, she could make out another lady seated at the counter. Inside the store smelled of roses; hundreds of clothes for both men and women were lined up in rows which seemed to extend forever.

As she approached the store counter, the lady looked up to regard her; Andonia could see that the woman wasn't really a lady at all. She was rather old, with a wrinkled up face that seemed to stare at her longingly. The old woman also had a pair of reading glasses on, and Andonia could see that she had been reading a magazine.

"Hello, how may I be of service to you?" Her voice was cordial and amiable.

"I need dress," Andonia said quickly, pointing towards the dress at the show-glass she had seen outside.

"Oh, that, dress…?" the old woman asked. "It's barely just came in my last stock, about two days ago. It's really nice, right?"

Andonia only nodded her head slowly. The old woman didn't look like some petty employed cashier, and she soon realized that she was probably talking directly to the store owner.

"That's great. Trust me, it's the perfect dress if you're going on a date with someone really special, if you know what I mean," she dropped a wink at Andonia and headed towards the show-glass.

Within seconds, she was soon back with the dress, which she placed on the counter.

"Even though I'd say that we have about several of this in the stock, I'd like you to have the one you saw in the show-glass. Yeah, it was, after all, the only thing that caught your attention when you were passing by," the old woman said.

"Si… I like it," Andonia replied. Then she paused a bit and asked, "How much?"

The old woman's face brightened up, "Why not try it on first? And if it's not a perfect fit, I'll let you have it at whatever price you want; and if it is, I'll still give a whooping discount."

"Gracias…" Andonia said quite grateful.

They headed towards the dressing room, which had a large mirror mounted in place, and with the help of the store owner, got into the red dress.

It was a perfect fit. The dress flowed down like a fountain of red wine and swept the linoleum floor as she glanced at herself in the mirror.

"You look so beautiful," the old store owner complimented. "Would you be having the dress?"

Andonia shook her head rapidly in agreement. She could already envision Jonas' face filled with wonder, admiration and maybe love as she would walk down the stairs which led up to her family house. She wondered if he would kiss her, and the thought of that made her heart race faster than a sports car.

"Hello, would you be paying cash or you have a card?" the old woman asked.

"Cash..." she muttered, "How much…?"

"That'd be about thirty dollars and sixteen cents. But I'll accept thirty dollars," the old woman replied.

Andonia nodded her head in understanding. She had only fifty dollars, which she had worked for almost fourteen hours to earn, but it was worth it anyway. She was going to have the dress.

She slipped her hand slowly into her purse, which was concealed in her hand bag, and took out thirty dollars which she handed to the old store owner.

"Thanks, let's have the dress packaged and the receipt issued, shall we?" the old store owner beckoned.

Andonia said nothing. But followed almost as if in a trance; she was already dreaming about the dinner tonight.

* * *

"Damn! You look quite great!" Rick exclaimed, checking out Jonas who was clad in his suit. "Like, I'd do you for free if I was a girl."

"Thanks for the compliments, Rick. But, no thanks," Jonas replied, adjusting his bowtie. "I guess I'm set to go. Mind if I borrow the Benz?"

"I don't mind. It's your night, man. Enjoy it totally and whatever you do -- don't dabble into any sort of religious talk with her. Mexicans generally have a strong sense of religion," Rick advised, throwing Jonas the keys of the requested car.

"Really…? Is that a fact? Or you're just kidding as usual," he asked.

"Not really, but I have had a direct experience with one and it didn't go too well, so just try to be as careful as possible. If she initiates any religious talk, evade it or lie," Rick pointed out thoughtfully.

"But why would I lie in regards to my own opinion? Not that I have any issues with Christians as people, but I don't buy the whole God and Jesus Christ thing," Jonas affirmed.

"Yeah, but just try to enjoy yourself. It might not even come up, but if it does, tread carefully; Mexicans are very religious, especially to the Catholic Faith."

"Okay then, see you, Rick," Jonas said, picking up the keys and heading towards the garage. The Benz, which was among at least nine other cars in Rick's exquisite garage, was probably one of the best cars in the fleet.

As the car glided out of the garage into the driveway, Jonas thought about Rick's advice. There was the fact that Mexicans were indeed religious people, but there was no need to generalize. If she was religious, he would know. In the long run, it wasn't really going to be a problem – as long as she was willing to cut him some slack if the relationship eventually led to marriage.

The car moved with ease out into Third Lane and took the direct exit, which led directly from Claremont to Hovels March. His heart was thumping in his chest steadily and rhythmically. But he wasn't going to appear queasy when he finally saw her, he assured himself.

* * *

She admired herself in the mirror. Indeed, the old store owner had been quite right -- she was looking absolutely breathtaking. Her mother had kept casting furtive glances at her as she prepared the evening meal for the family.

Her father wasn't home; he had traveled down to New Mexico across the border to transport coffee alongside with her brothers. She stared at herself in the mirror and wondered what his reaction would be like.

These thoughts were, however, interrupted by a loud knocking on her door; she had done well to keep the door locked because her mother kept passing silly comments, but it sounded very urgent now.

Glancing at the wall clock, which had a picture of Christ on the Cross emboldened on it, she could tell that it was almost 8:00pm. She hurried to the door and unlocked it quickly.

There stood her mother with a look of contempt scrambling up the features of her face. "The American," was all she said as she moved away from Andonia and headed back to the kitchen.

Her heart almost jumped into her mouth as she hurried to get prepared; she hastily put on her shoes, dabbed on some powder and applied some gloss on her lips. Heaving a huge sigh, she went down the stairs, holding up her gown like a newly wedded bride.

Even though her responses had been cold, the woman whom Jonas had deducted could be Andonia's mother had offered him a seat. It was a creaky old chair which was directly behind the flight of stairs, which led up to the upper floor of the house. He could only guess that her mother was generally hostile towards Americans; that wasn't something new, most Mexicans were.

The footfalls, which fell heavily, were light and steep. He turned around slowly, and his breathing ceased.

She must be some goddess, he thought to himself. The red gown only added to her grace, beauty and nobility. Her jet-black hair flowed down to the very reaches of her shoulder, and her lips sparkled. For a moment, Jonas couldn't talk.

"Hallo, Jonas, estas listo?" she asked brightly.

He tried to reply but the words were sort of caught up in his mouth.

"Jonas…?"

"Oh, sorry, I don't even know what to say. You look stunning," Jonas said, still awe-struck.

"Gracias..." she replied smiling.

"Okay, I guess we can go. I hope your mum –" Jonas continued, but she simply cut him short by placing a finger on his lips. That gesture sent a thrill throughout his body making him shiver with excitement.

"Let's go," she whispered.

Jonas only nodded.

"Hasta luego, Madre," she called to her mother but was replied by a simple grunt which came from the kitchen.

Holding her hand felt quite comforting as he led her out of the house, straight into the driveway where the Benz was parked. She didn't even swoon or compliment the car, which would have been something any young American woman would've done. She simply allowed Jonas to open the passenger's door for her, and she sat down quietly.

After they were both ready, Jonas started the car and they were soon on their way to the Grand Royale.

6 CHAPTER SIX

The restaurant, by all means, lived up to its name. It was indeed grand. When Rick had recommended Grand Royale, Jonas had not totally doubted him – it was, after all, one of the few perks of being a millionaire. Your taste was most certainly going to be quite high.

As soon as they stepped into the restaurant, they were waylaid by ushers, two girls dressed smartly in white shirts over black skirts. The ushers directed them to a table which was just at the window overlooking the city.

People were seated at their various tables, chattering and having small talks over glasses filled with expensive wine. Each table was lit up with red candles, which stood on gold candlesticks, and just above was an exquisite chandelier over each table.

After they had been seated, a waiter dressed in a suit approached their table with menus clutched fast in his grip. He smiled warmly at Jonas and Andonia. who was seated perfectly at the other end of the table.

"What would you like us to start you on, sir?" He was most certainly an ebullient fellow, Jonas thought; he was absolutely good at his job.

"Would you be kind to get us some champagne first, and we'll get back to you as soon as we have gone through the menu," Jonas replied. The waiter nodded his head in understanding and proceeded to get their order.

"What do you think about this place?" Jonas asked, smiling at her.

"Good," she replied. "Beautiful," she further added.

"Well, this is actually my first time here too. Rick recommended it. I think it's rather nice," he paused, regarding her. "Would you be obliged to teach me Mexican Spanish sometime?"

She looked at him wide-eyed and laughed softly. "Si, I teach you, but one thing," she finally replied.

"And what might that be?" Jonas furthered enthusiastically.

"You teach me Inglés too," she replied.

"Certainly," he asserted, smiling. "English is really not that complicated if you actually get around to it. I think it's actually the most easiest language to comprehend."

Andonia only shrugged, still looking at him.

Consequently, the waiter approached their table once more. "I hope you're having a lovely evening, sir. Have you finally decided on what you're going to have?" he asked.

"Of course," Jonas replied. "I'll have your French toast, steak and chops," he glanced at Andonia, "Did you see anything you'd like on the menu?"

Andonia nodded her head, took the menu up and pointed at it. And the waiter squinted closely to regard what was being pointed at.

"Oh, our famous Mexican course meal. That's a favorite." He smiled cheerfully and went about the business of getting the orders ready.

"You picked a Mexican dish?" Jonas asked.

"Si. I like Mexican food," she replied almost immediately. "America eat junk."

Jonas looked on at her blankly, then what she had said finally had some sort of meaning in his head. She had ordered Mexican food because she felt American food was really just junk food.

"That's fine. I guess you're kind of right in a way," Jonas agreed. "So, that was your mother I met back at home?"

She nodded her head in affirmation. "Si, Madre."

"And how about your father? Not forgetting your brothers, I didn't think I saw any of them back at home when I visited," Jonas noted.

"Pappy not home. Mexico, to get coffee," she replied.

"Oh, Pappy means father?" Jonas furthered.

"Si, Pappy or Papito," she asserted. A large trolley was being rolled towards their table. Dishes made of authentic silverware were crammed up on the trolley, which was being wheeled towards them by two waiters.

"Here comes our meal. I hope you enjoy it greatly," Jonas announced, but she only smiled shyly.

The waiters placed each dish on the table, taking care not to mix up the orders which had been taken earlier. As requested, Jonas was served French toast alongside with steak that was still quite hot.

Without thinking twice about it, he took one of the knives which was arranged in the assigned cutlery, sliced a huge chunk of steak, stabbed at it with his fork and popped it into his mouth. He repeated this sequence; over and over without looking up.

When he had half expected that the meal should be halfway or thereabouts, he reached out to grab a glass of wine when he paused looking at Andonia.

Her eyes were closed as if lost in some kind of holy convention; her lips were moving slowly and silently -- she was most certainly praying.

He looked on in awe mixed with astonishment at her. She had not touched her meal yet, and he had been already halfway through his. Heck, he was almost done with the damned food.

He swallowed the morsel of food which he had been chewing and leaned back on his chair, watching her closely.

After she was done with the Lord's Prayer, just as she had been taught by her abuela, she opened her eyes and smiled warmly at Jonas.

"I pray before I eat," she mumbled, silently flushing a bit.

"That's fine," Jonas replied. "I was kind of just captivated by your devotion and sense of religion, so what was the prayer?"

"Apostles' Creed," she stated. "I go to church back then with my abuela."

"What's that? Some sort of toy?"

She giggled loudly at that. "No. My grandmother, dead now."

Jonas nodded his head slowly, "I honestly wish I could get to know you better."

She dropped her spoon and extended her hand towards him just across the table. Her hand felt as smooth as marble, and as soft as silk; almost so refreshing and sweet.

"Si. I tell you all about myself."

"Good, so where are you exactly from," Jonas started. "I know you're Mexican, but I wanna know if you're deeply rooted in your origin."

"Born in Mexico. Pappy from Spain and Madre from Mexico. Thirty-six and single," Andonia replied.

"Oh, so you're half Spanish and half Mexican?" he asked.

She nodded her head in reply.

"Well, I'm a full-blooded American, I was born and brought up across the Eastern Seaboard, and I presently work as a financial auditor," Jonas declared.

Music soon filled up the room, which had been otherwise quiet except for the chit-chats of other people seated at their various tables and the hustle and bustle of waiters delivering the meals as soon possible.

"I really like you, Andonia," Jonas suddenly said. The thought had been nagging at him, rearing up like heads of the mythological Hydra. But he had been cutting it off; it would be totally crazy if he had told her he actually loved her on the first date, he felt it would be absurd.

"I sell Mexican food back in restaurante, but want to study," she said, and quickly added, "Te quiero mucho."

"What does that actually mean?" His curiosity had known no bounds, as usual.

"It mean: love you or like you," she smiled. She was already halfway through her meal. After the meal was done, Jonas told her all about his old marriage; he skipped no part at all.

She had listened quite enraptured and enthralled. "So sorry," she whispered after he was done. It had been a long time again since he had never felt the kind of guilt he wasn't feeling after the incident had happened.

"I know you enjoy jogging, but do you have other hobbies? Like swimming, touring, mountain climbing," Jonas asked. "I really want to know."

"Cooking," she muttered under her breath, "I cooking good food a lot."

"You actually mean: I cook a lot of good food," Jonas said. "I guess we're finally making some headway."

Andonia laughed heartily as the main dessert was brought to them; she was really having one of the most swell times of her life. But she had noticed that Jonas hadn't prayed before eating. Not that it had mattered at first -- he was first and foremost, after all, an American. And most Americans had a liberal inclination towards religion. But not Andonia.

Religion wasn't just something that could be done at anytime one liked for her; it was one of the very backbones of her family. She could still remember visiting her abuela when she had been very young, perhaps about six or seven. The old woman always propped her up on her lap and taught little Andonia how to read the Rosary. Her abuela had gotten her a small rosary, which she had always worn around her neck proudly. And at age ten, she could recite almost all the parts of the rosary, taking time to hold each bead accordingly.

"You seem lost in deep thought," Jonas observed. "Is something wrong?"

She shook her head in the negative, snapping out of her silent reverie. "No, everything okay."

"So, talking about Mexican Spanish, how does one say: you're beautiful?" Jonas inquired.

"Eres hermosa," she replied smiling. "Am beautiful?" she added, it wasn't supposed to sound like a question, but it had come out that way all the same.

"If I could explain how you look right now in words, I could ramble on forever. Andonia, your beauty is inexplicable; almost like a mystery that is shrouded," Jonas said.

This only made her smile all the more, "Thank you, I know-how."

"Okay, that was supposed to be: 'Thank you, I now know.' I guess if you're gonna be teaching me Spanish, I could as well teach you English."

They suddenly fell silent.

He watched as she sipped the wine. She caught his gaze, blushed a little as a smile broke across her face. He was starting to just love watching her. A voyeur looking into a secret world.

He smiled warmly back, as if to comfort her. It actually did, in a way, and she was beginning to enjoy his gaze. Soaking it in. Feeling his eyes move over her. From her eyes to her nose, cheeks, lips.

The curve of her neck, the very slope of her shoulders, and her chest. The tiny bit of cleavage just peeking out from her dress. Again, she blushed, but this time, so does he.

They locked eyes across the table. Everything around them seemed to fade away. They were in a universe all their own. Lost in the depths of each other's eyes. She could feel his desire; he, hers. But it was not lustful. It was however calm, gentle, and controlled, with a sense of longing to escape forever into that universe around them.

They barely noticed the waiter as he placed the dessert in front of them. A simple plate of fruit and cheese. He watched her eat, calmly bringing each morsel to her lips. He marveled at the pleasure she took from each bite. Her face amazingly expressive. Every bite as if she was tasting for the first time.

She gazed at him, yet again, over her glass as she sipped her wine. She knew he was watching her. She slipped a grape between her lips. Smiling coyly as her teeth crushed the skin, exploding the juices into her mouth. She reached for a strawberry. He deliberately reached out to it too, just as her fingertip touch the ripened fruit. He grinned, taking a large bite. She offered the most convincing pout. He smiled affectionately and fed her the rest. Her eyes smiled back at him.

They went on. Refilling their wine glasses and eating slowly. Just enough to keep the wine from going to their heads. They did not speak. Time stood still, stopping just for them. An eternity to enjoy each other's company. He watching her. She being watched.

Anyone could see the energy between them. It could be felt. Something surreal was happening at that table. To them, it was completely natural, existing at that moment in their own universe.

Sipping wine throughout. Savoring the unique yet complimentary flavors. They ate in silence. Feasting off each other's forks until hardly anything was left. Their meals devoured.

Their bellies growing heavy. Their appetites nearly satiated. A single dessert to share. A single spoon. He fed her a small bite. Creamy and rich. She couldn't help but smile with pleasure at the sweetness. Her innocent pleasure made its way across the tiny table, straight into his heart. How could he not help but love her? He took a large bite with the enthusiasm of a child. She laughed quietly at his playfulness.

Another bite for her, larger than the first. Some was left on her lips. He planned that, of course. She knew it. He reaches out towards her before she can raise her napkin. But his reach is not for her lips. He proceeded to put his hand softly on her cheek and leaned towards her. She responded likewise, and he kisses her softly.

Tasting the sweetness of the dessert mixed with the sweetness of her. Everything around them faded away. They were in their own universe. Locked in a kiss. Time stood still.

She broke the kiss and looked into his eyes; her heart felt quite heavy. She was in love with him. It was hard to explain, but it was absolutely true.

"That -- was absolutely incredible," Jonas heard himself say.

She only smiled at him. "Si. It is," she whispered. "Queiro ir a casa."

"What's that?" he asked.

"Home, Madre wait for me, late," she replied.

"Right. I'll drive you," he answered, calling for the waiter, who strode briskly towards them with the bill. After it had been duly paid for, Jonas led her out of the restaurant and straight towards the parked Benz.

"So, when do we start our lessons?" he asked wistfully.

"Anytime. Remember, you teach me Inglés too," she said.

"Of course, I guess it's trade by barter then," he winked at her; this made her giggle for a while. He opened the passenger's side for her, and after they were both belted in, started the car and drove off with the full silvery moon just overhead in the clear night sky.

7 CHAPTER SEVEN

Days turned slowly into months and their bond grew stronger.
The language barrier was becoming less noticeable. Jonas had taken
his time to teach her the intricacies of the English Language; starting
with parts of speech, sentence constructions and the use of past and
present tenses. And she, in turn, had taught him how to say simple
words, numbers and objects in the Mexican language.

However, language wasn't the problem. It was something way
beyond that; something which threatened to tear their budding love
apart.

It had started casually, as a request. Jonas, who had had a successful
year at Rick's, decided it was time to get his own apartment in
Fairfax, which was just about a mile from Fairfield.

"It's a fairly large house, Rick. Maybe not as lush or exquisite as this
one, but certainly a way to start," Jonas said.

Rick furrowed his eyebrows and shook his head slowly. "C'mon,
man, why would you leave me all alone? I greatly suspect this to be
the doing of your new Mexican girlfriend. I guess -- privacy and all."

Jonas chuckled softly. "That's totally buzzkill. We both knew I'd
have to move out sometime."

"I surmise this has to do with that recent promotion I gave you back at the office," Rick muttered grimly. To be quite candid, he had grown used to Jonas' company.

"Yeah, c'mon, Rick. Fairfax is just a mile away, and besides, I'll still be coming here every other weekend."

"Okay. So, where exactly in Fairfax?"

"Just past Nick's gas station," Jonas replied. "I haven't informed Donia yet, and I was kinda hoping she'd come there to see me more often before I propose to her."

"You're thinking of proposing?" Rick asked. "Wow, I never thought it would eventually come to this. I'm just speechless."

"Same here, Ricky. But I have gotten the ring. I figured, why not start afresh with something new, anything that portends a new beginning; so I skipped giving her my grandmother's ring, which Melissa sent back to me through the mail, and bought this instead." He brought out a small box wrapped with a red ribbon.

Rick nodded slowly, patting him on the back. "This is great news, man."

And that had been about a week ago. He had called Andonia and informed her of the change. Although, he always suspected that she was always avoiding coming to see him -- probably due to the fact that he was residing with Rick -- but things had taken a new turn after he had met her as usual at Grand Royale, which had, in fact, turned out to be their meeting point.

"I don't really get it Donia, why won't you come and see me? I'm not even staying at Rick's anymore," Jonas complained. This had become one of the few topics that they never seemed to have an agreement on; they'd drag on it back and forth. But she always remained obstinate.

"No es asi, Jonas, I can't just stay out of the house anytime I like. Madre would be mad with me," Andonia replied.

"C'mon, Donia, you're almost thirty-six! Don't tell me your mother would be bothered if you're in the house of a guy you're hoping to marry," he whispered sharply. At such times, it was always hard to comprehend. The hold that her family had over her was sometimes infuriating and at the same time incredible.

"I'm a Mexican woman. I can't sleep under the roof of another man that I'm not married to. Trata de entenderme, Jonas."

"I'm trying to understand you. I have been trying to ever since I fell in love with you. So, what happens after we're married? Would you still be bound to your family?"

"Family is everything. My brother Carlos married his wife, and they're still living not quite far from us. I always want to be close to my pappy and madre. It's just a Mexican thing. I know it's hard to explain," Andonia furthered, pausing each time to regard Jonas' countenance, which had grown quite grave.

"So, even if we get married, we would still have to live close by to your family? That sounds absolutely ridiculous," Jonas grunted.

She only fell silent, looking down at her hands. He had never raised his voice against her before, and he was doing it now.

"Damisela..." he started soothingly, "I don't mean to sound cruel, nor did I mean to raise my voice, but try to see reason. Think about it this way. What if I was posted to another state in the country? Maybe Alabama or Minnesota or even Florida? And we're married. Would you insist on being close to your family? For Christ's sake, Fairfax is barely a mile from Fairfield, and all I'm asking for is weekends."

"Don't do that again," she chided.

He gawked at her, rather confused. "Do what?"

"No uses el nombre de Cristo en vano. It's very bad," she said, looking defiantly at him.

"Okay... Okay... Sorry about that. But you do understand me, don't you? Entiendes mi pinto?"

"Entiendes mi punto," she corrected his wrong use of the word. "I understand what you mean, Jonas." She reached out and took both his hands into hers. "I love you. I really do, but I don't know if things would work out for you and I."

"And why's that?" he asked quietly.

"It's quite clear, Jonas. These few months have been an exhilarating experience for me. I never thought I'd be happy until I met you. Everything I have ever wanted in a man, I found in you. I really love you but --" she paused, a single tear formed at a corner in her eye and cascaded down her cheek.

"But what?" he asked; his heart was racing rather fast.

"You're not Christian. You don't go to church. I doubt if you believe in God. And there's the fact that you're an American, Los estadounidenses realmente no valoran la familia," Andonia stated.

"I totally disagree with you. Americans do have a sense of family, but not necessarily fanatical about it like Mexicans. I hate to state it that way, but it's the truth," Jonas replied.

She sighed heavily and looked away lost in deep thought. Her face, which had been lively, crumbled into a picturesque of sadness.

Jonas tried to hold her hand again, but she cringed back at his touch. Perhaps, he had taken it too far, he thought to himself -- after all, everyone had their own cultural differences. But such things were supposed to be secondary to the fact they were in love with each other.

"I go home," she said with a note of finality. "Talk to you later."

Jonas gripped her hand tightly and held on. Some other people in the restaurant turned to gape at them, but he was completely oblivious of that fact.

"I know you're angry. But that's just the truth, Donia. Don't allow petty things to destroy what we have. I really love you," he managed to croak.

She shrugged him off and walked out of the restaurant. He just stood there watching her go, like he had done several months before, back on the bridge.

He suddenly felt sad. The sadness engulfed him, tearing his insides apart like ripped paper.

The wine he had ordered was left unopened on the table after he had paid the bill and dropped a tip for the waiter.

They didn't talk for another three weeks.

* * *

"You'll have to talk to her sometime," Rick postulated. "From all you have just said, none of you are actually at fault. This is just a minor issue."

"And that was exactly my point, Ricky. But she wasn't seeing things my way. I don't really get it. Why would someone want to always stay very close to their family? Heck! I hadn't seen Kye in almost fifteen years, since he enlisted until he turned up on our front porch about some months ago. Same goes for Mason, who I finally saw at the anniversary of my father. This doesn't mean we don't care about each other, but things happen -- we're now grown up men. If I wanted to talk to them, I could always call or send a postcard. How hard is that?" Jonas asked bitterly.

"You could say that, when the average American gets his first ride, he hops on it when he's eighteen and drives out of his family forever. I don't think it's the same with Mexicans, Jonas. I know very little about their culture, but I do know they value family above everything else. Asking her to simply go with you, without any regard for her family, was a bit extreme," Rick replied.

"So, what are your suggestions, Ricky? I need her back. She won't pick my calls. I have sent her several messages too, which remain unread. I doubt if she's even going to reply them."

"I suggest that you get to know her family, Jonas, get to understand her culture and, most importantly, make her know that everything about her matters and that you care."

Jonas glanced at Rick in shock. "I can't even believe it's you saying all these things, old boy. I mean, I was expecting you to give bad advice."

They both laughed heartily at that, and Jonas promised Rick he would see if he could try contacting her again.

8 CHAPTER EIGHT

His messages kept coming and coming in a ceaseless loop. But she had decided that she wasn't ready to talk to him, at least not just yet.

For the past few days, she had been ruminating, brooding and, of course, weighing her options.

He had nearly pushed her to the wall. But was it really his fault or hers? She wondered balefully. Of course there was no one to blame.

But she wasn't going to just act like what he had said back at the restaurant hadn't gotten to her. All of her life, she had always known her family -- perhaps, she was now at that dreaded crossroad where she had to choose between her love for Jonas and her never-ending commitment to her family.

She sobbed silently. Her face, which was always bright, was crestfallen with gloom, which seemed to radiate from her towards her pappy and madre.

"Hay algo mal, Andonia?" Her pappy had asked, noticing her dark countenance. "Is this about the Americano?"

She had forced a smile. "No pappy, everything's fine." Her

response, which was quite untrue, felt a little bit comforting. She was going to lose Jonas, and she certainly hoped she had the courage to go through with it.

Her reflection on the mirror just on the dresser was a pitiable version of her old self. Eyes swollen from long hours of endless tears, lips dried out and cracked, her skin which always glowed had seemed to lose their light. She felt hollow. Helplessly empty.

She had this vague unrelenting feeling that he was going to finally send her a voicemail. A rather long, lengthy voicemail that would go like:

Hello, Andonia, this is Jonas. I know this is going to be very hard, but I guess I have done all I can. I really do love you. But it appears you love your family more, so I guess that ends it for us. I can only wish you all the best and hope you find that man who would be perfect for you. Clearly, I'm not that man. I guess all I can do is wish you well and hope you move forward without me.

GOODBYE.

This brief imagined voicemail message played through her head like some broken record on an old gramophone.

It sounded terrifying and horrible to her imaginary ears and she only sobbed heavily. Couldn't he see that she was in a dilemma? Couldn't he see that all she wanted was to be with him? To stay wrapped in his warm embrace, kissing him, feeling him and intermingling their souls together in conjugal bliss. Her eyes were drained of tears.

She allowed herself to fall back on the bed.

Her energy was far spent. She could feel sleep eluding her. Yet, she couldn't bring herself to sleep.

But still, she was taken on the wings of oblivion and her eyes, which were heavy, gradually eased her away into a Dreamworld.

In that Dreamworld, Jonas was there. He was clad in a white suit, and his face was illuminated by a thousand bright lights. His right hand was extended towards her, beckoning her on.

She looked down at her feet; wild roses were littered on the path which led towards him; he was standing with a man dressed in a cassock. She could make out her family, just among the unknown faces of the people invited. Glancing around, she was soon aware that she was also wearing a gown, a white wedding gown which sparkled like polished silver.

Their hands connected and a voice tore through the veil of her dream.

"Andonia..." her mother nudged her lightly. "Alguien aqui para verte, the American."

Her eyes fluttered open slowly and she could make out the blurred face of her mother. Then, suddenly, she sat up almost immediately.

"Jonas?" she asked doubtfully.

"Si. Jonas," her mother replied, nodding her head in affirmation.

"But --" Andonia started and stopped short when she heard laughter float upwards from the living room. It was a laughter that she had heard before, one of cheerfulness mixed with sudden vivacious energy.

She sprang up from her bed and rushed past her mother, clambering down the stairs so fast that she almost slipped on the third landing.

There he was seated with her pappy. He was clad in a flannel shirt over a pair of jeans. Her pappy was pouring him a glass of tequila and he was just saying "Gracias, senor" over and over in a cute manner which made her also burst into laughter.

He turned to see her standing there and scrambled up hastily. Within seconds, they were caught in each other's arms, and right in front of her pappy, who didn't seem to mind.

He didn't say anything. There was really nothing to say at first. After they disengaged from each other, he proceeded to kiss her softly. Their lips merged together slowly and he savoured the taste of her mouth. Exploring the hidden corners with his tongue, they were completely oblivious of everything that was going on around them.

"I'm sorry," he whispered finally. "I'm so sorry, Donia."

"I'm sorry too. But I love you, Jonas, more than anything in the world. But I also love my family; my pappy, my madre and brothers. I know --"

He cut her short by placing a finger on her lips. "Everything will work itself out with time. Everything will be fine, there's always going to be a way."

"Si. I guessed so," she responded.

He laughed, softly stroking her hair. "You still got that past tense factor," he winked at her, and she punched at him playfully.

She turned to see her pappy and madre smiling at them. And she hurried and hugged the both of them.

She didn't, of course, see that Jonas had slipped his hand slowly into his jeans pocket and procured the box. She didn't see that he was already on one knee waiting for her to turn around. She didn't see the look of astonishment scribbled on the face of her parents.

It was only when her mother gasped with surprise, did she turn around. Then she gasped too.

He was on one knee holding up a diamond ring; the smile on his face was genuine and also filled with love.

"Andonia Moreno," he said. "Would you do me the honor of being my wife and partner? Would you make me the happiest man on Earth?"

Tears cascaded her cheeks. But it wasn't the fact that he had proposed to her. But his selfless act; he had finally agreed to be part of her family. Something which must have taken him a lot of effort.

She moved towards him and embraced him. The ring, which was still in his hand, was slipped on quickly, and then she kissed him again and was only taken back to reality when she heard everyone, including her parents, applauding them.

9 EPILOGUE

The wedding date was fixed, and Jonas was eagerly looking forward to it. Rick had decided that they would do it by the lake on his luxury yacht.

"Don't kill my vibe, man! It's a great idea, and since I'd be best man, I guess I could always suggest suitable venues," Rick protested.

"I don't think the lake's a good idea, man. But whatever. It's not that bad anyway," Jonas said.

"Yeah, I hope we'll be getting lots of whiskey and Wild Turkey's. Those things are crazy, and we have to celebrate to you, Jonas."

"No drinking, Rick."

"Total Buzzkill. You just keep killing the vibe. I hope Donia dumps your ass on that day."

"Not on your life sucker."

"Gotcha."

"So, how about Suzzy? I thought you two were hitting it off," Jonas asked.

"You know how I am. Besides, Suzzy is really a great girl. No need trying to break her heart and ruin her fine makeup."

"Yeah, you'll never change, buster."

"And you too."

"I better get these wedding invitations mailed to Mason and Kye. I'm pretty sure they'll be more than happy to come."

"Yeah, I guess so. How about Donia?"

"Probably testing her wedding dress. You have to see it Rick. It's as white as silver and very pure."

"Nice. I guess I told you, Jonas, good things would always come our way."

"I guess so too, they always will."

ABOUT THE AUTHOR

Mimi Burbank enjoys writing sensual romance & suspenseful love stories. Please remember to leave this book 5 stars if you enjoyed it!

www.ingramcontent.com/pod-product-compliance
Lightning Source LLC
Chambersburg PA
CBHW061526020726

47502CB00006B/2253